Robin Hood

adapted by Annie Ingle
illustrated by Domenick D'Andrea

A STEPPING STONE BOOK™

Random House 🏠 New York

CURR
P2
7
.I685
.Ro
2005

Text copyright © 1991 by Random House, Inc. Illustrations copyright © 1991 by Domenick D'Andrea. Cover illustration copyright © 2005 by Robert Hunt. All rights reserved under International and Pan-American Copyright Conventions. Published in the United States by Random House Children's Books, a division of Random House, Inc., New York, and simultaneously in Canada by Random House of Canada Limited, Toronto. Originally published as a Bullseye Step into Classics book by Random House, Inc., in 1991.

www.steppingstonesbooks.com

Library of Congress Cataloging-in-Publication Data
Ingle, Annie.
Robin Hood / adapted by Annie Ingle ; illustrated by Domenick D'Andrea ; cover illustration by Robert Hunt.
    p.   cm.
"A Stepping Stone book."
SUMMARY: Robin Hood, Maid Marian, and the merry outlaws of Sherwood Forest repeatedly outwit the Sheriff of Nottingham and befriend the poor.
ISBN 0-679-81045-5 (pbk.) — ISBN 0-679-91045-X (lib. bdg.)
1. Robin Hood (Legendary character)—Legends. [1. Robin Hood (Legendary character)—Legends. 2. Folklore—England.] I. D'Andrea, Domenick, ill.
II. Pyle, Howard, 1853–1911. Merry adventures of Robin Hood. III. Title.
PZ8.1.I685Ro 2005   [398.2]—dc22   2004017641

Printed in the United States of America   32 31 30 29 28 27 26 25

Contents

The Making of an Outlaw

These adventures took place many years ago in merry old England. Richard the Lion-Hearted ruled the land.

One May morning a lad from the town of Locksley set out for the fair at Nottingham. He carried a bow and arrows. He was eager to compete in the shooting match at the fair.

But he never got there.

A man stopped him on the way there. This man thought he would have a little fun at the expense of a young lad.

He challenged the lad to a private shooting match. The lad agreed. And he beat the man. Fair and square.

But the man was angry. And embarrassed. What if word got out that he had been beaten? And by a mere lad? He tried to kill the lad. The lad struck back, killing the man.

The Sheriff of Nottingham offered one thousand gold pieces as a reward for the lad from Locksley.

The lad went into hiding in Sherwood Forest. There he lived the life of an outlaw for many years.

But he was no ordinary outlaw.

Like most outlaws, he stole. But only from the rich. He kept no more than he needed. He gave the rest to the poor.

These were especially trying times for the poor. King Richard was a good man. But he had gone to fight in the Crusades. He left England in the hands of men who were not so good. Men like the Sheriff of Nottingham and many of the Church's bishops. These bad men got richer and richer. Meanwhile, the poor only got poorer.

Only one man looked after the poor—the outlaw who lived in Sherwood Forest. He became a hero in his own time. And a legend in ours.

His name? Robin Hood!

Many stories about Robin Hood have been handed down. Are they true? Read them and judge for yourself.

One

The Meeting on the Bridge

It was a golden morning in Sherwood Forest. Robin Hood was looking for adventure. Soon he came to a wide rushing river. A very narrow bridge ran across it. On the other side of the bridge stood a tall stranger. He held a stout staff.

"Stand back, stranger!" shouted Robin. "Let the better man cross first!"

"Stand back yourself," said the stranger. "For I am that better man."

"Not with a bow," said Robin. For Robin knew he was the best bowman in all of England.

"Touch that bow and I'll tan your hide," the stranger snarled.

"Just try it," said Robin. "And I'll part your mangy hair with an arrow."

"You're nothing but a coward," said the stranger. "You with your fancy bow. And me with my humble staff."

Now, Robin hated being called a coward. He laid down his bow. Then he cut and trimmed a stout branch for a staff. Meanwhile, he sized up the other man.

Robin was tall. But this man was a full head taller. And far broader. But I'll beat him anyway, Robin thought. For Robin was brave and sure of his skills as a fighter.

Both men stepped onto the bridge. The two men were well matched. They traded blow for blow. At last Robin jabbed the stranger in the ribs. The stranger staggered. Then he hauled off and cracked Robin's head.

Robin saw stars.

When the stars faded, Robin was mad! He lunged at the stranger.

But the tall man simply stepped aside.

Splash! Robin tumbled headlong into the river.

"And where are you now, my good man?" The tall stranger roared with laughter.

Robin sputtered. Robin scowled. But the scowl soon turned merry. Even he had to admit it: He was a funny sight. Soon they both were laughing as Robin waded ashore.

"Let's shake," said Robin. "For you are the better man. With that staff, at least."

"And you took your dunking like a sport," said the stranger. They shook hands. "What is your name?"

"Some men call me Robin Hood."

The stranger's mouth fell open. "You? The famous Robin Hood? Who steals from the rich and gives to the poor?"

"The same." Robin laughed. "Only I do keep a bit for myself and my men."

"May I be one of your men?" asked the stranger. "There is no man in all of England I would rather serve."

Robin stroked his golden beard. "I can always use another good man. What is your name?"

"John Little."

"John Little, eh?" Robin's blue eyes twinkled. He lifted a silver horn. He blew into it three times.

Soon the woods came alive with men. Like Robin, they were dressed all in forest green.

"Fellows!" Robin called out to them. "Meet the newest member of our merry band. His name is John Little. But I say Little John suits him far better. For as you can see, he is anything but!"

Everyone shouted with laughter at Robin's joke. Even Little John.

Still laughing, they trooped deeper into the forest. Their hideout was beneath a huge oak tree.

It was an amazing place. They had made huts out of tree bark. Couches out of animal skins. And a vault for their treasures in the rocks nearby.

That night they made a great fire. What a feast they had! Fresh deer meat and wild duck. Green onions and fresh baked bread.

Afterward they enjoyed a bit of target practice. They used a wreath of flowers for a target. Robin Hood's

arrows always hit inside the wreath. Little John was impressed. And glad he was now one of Robin's merry men.

Then they lay on the soft moss. They sang songs by firelight. They told stories. They laughed and joked. Finally they fell asleep beneath the stars.

And so it was that Little John came to be Robin Hood's right-hand man. And his best friend in the whole world. Next to Maid Marian, of course.

Two

The Unhappy Bride

Marian's mother and Robin's mother had been best friends as girls. Robin's mother had married a woodsman out of love. Marian's mother had married a nobleman for his money. But the two women continued to be friends. Their two children grew up side by side.

When Robin first went to hide in Sherwood Forest, Marian found him. She vowed to remain his friend.

Robin thought this was dangerous. But Marian was as stubborn as Robin. And she knew the forest as well as he did.

Marian missed Robin. Whenever she could, she would steal away and go to the forest. There she dressed in forest green, just like the others. And she could shoot a bow as well as the best of them.

One fine day Robin and Marian strolled through the forest. Robin looked at Marian. She seemed sad.

"What is the matter?" he asked.

Marian frowned. "It is my friend Ellen. Tomorrow her father will make her marry a man she does not love."

"How unfair!" Robin shook his head.

"The man is very old and very

rich," said Marian. "And her father needs the money."

"People should marry for love," said Robin. "Like my parents."

"Yes," said Marian. "I agree. That is why I thought . . ." But she did not finish.

"What did you think?" Robin asked.

"Oh, nothing! You probably would not want to do it."

"You will never know unless you ask," said Robin.

"I was thinking," Marian said. "Maybe you could rescue Ellen from this marriage."

Robin thought for a bit. Finally he said, "No. The Sheriff would be angry with me. Besides, this marriage is none of my business."

Marian sighed. "I thought you would say that. I guess it does not matter that she is in love with another."

"Who?" Robin asked.

"One of your men."

"Which one?"

"Can't you guess?"

Robin thought. Little John seemed as merry as ever. Only this morning

Will Scarlet was whistling. Then there was his minstrel, Alan-a-Dale. Alan's songs had been rather sad lately.

"It's Alan, isn't it?" Robin said.

Marian smiled. "Yes!"

Robin turned back to the hideout. "This marriage must not take place."

The next day Robin dressed up in a disguise. He wore feathers and ribbons of many colors. He carried a harp in one hand. His silver horn hung from his belt. He was a musician.

Robin set off for the church with twenty of his best men. Little John, Will Scarlet, and Alan-a-Dale, of course. Friar Tuck also came.

Friar Tuck was a member of the band. But he was also a member of the Church. Robin needed a holy man to perform the wedding he had

in mind. The wedding of Alan and
Ellen.

Friar Tuck led a mule with three
bags of gold on its back.

The church was very grand. Most
of the men hid outside in the bushes.
Robin went inside. A couple of the
others sneaked in behind him. And
hid themselves well.

The Bishop was alone in the church. He wore a velvet cloak. Around his neck he wore a heavy gold chain.

Robin did not think much of this holy man who dressed in velvet and gold.

Robin said, "I am a harper with wonderful skills. Let me play at this wedding. I promise that the bride will fall madly in love with the man she marries."

Now, the Bishop knew that the bride did not love the groom. So he said, "That would be wonderful indeed. Do what you say, and I will pay whatever you ask. But let me hear you play first."

Robin shook his head. "Not until the happy couple arrive."

Just then the bride and groom entered the church. The groom's men followed.

"It is a deal," the Bishop whispered. But he was angry. He planned to pay the harper with a beating, not gold.

The bride's father entered next. His men followed.

The groom was gray-haired and stooped with age. He rubbed his hands together. He was very happy. Everyone was happy except the bride. Ellen was pale. She could not even look at the man she was to marry.

Bride and groom stepped up to the altar. The Bishop began.

But Robin stepped up to the altar too. He stood right between the bride and groom!

"Just look at this girl!" Robin said in a loud voice. "How pale she is! These are lilies in her cheeks. Not roses. This is not a fit wedding. A young girl to such an old man. And she does not even love him!"

No one breathed a word. Who knew what to say? Who knew where to look? It was as if everyone had turned to stone. Everyone except Robin Hood.

Robin put the silver horn to his lips and blew three times.

Little John and Will Scarlet jumped down from where they had been hiding. They stood on either side of Robin, swords ready.

"Here I am!" Friar Tuck called down from the organ loft. "Ready to perform the happy service."

"What is going on here?" The groom drew his sword. His men did the same.

The front doors flew open. Eighteen more men wearing forest green burst in. They were ready for battle. At the head of them was Alan-a-Dale.

Joyfully Ellen called out to her true love. "Alan!"

"Alan-a-Dale!" said Ellen's father. "So this is all your idea!"

"No," said Robin. "You have Robin Hood to thank." He bowed low.

The groom and his men put away their swords. They had all heard of Robin Hood. No one there wanted to fight him.

The old groom said to Ellen's father, "Why didn't you tell me your daughter loved another man? If she prefers him to me, I prefer to forget this wedding."

The proud old man left the church. His men followed.

Then Robin gave the three bags of gold to Ellen's father.

"This gold is yours if you give this marriage your blessing," said Robin.

Ellen's father was angry. But he needed the gold, so he blessed the marriage.

Then Friar Tuck married Alan-a-Dale and the fair Ellen. Never was there a happier couple!

Afterward the Bishop tried to sneak away.

"Wait!" called Robin. "You said if I caused the bride to love the groom, you would give me whatever I asked."

Robin was right. And the Bishop knew it. "What do you want?"

Robin stroked his beard. His eyes sparkled. "That gold chain you wear. Give it to the bride as a wedding gift."

The Bishop fumed. But in the end he gave the chain to Ellen.

A loud cheer went up.

The merry wedding band left the church. They returned to Sherwood Forest, where they had a splendid wedding feast.

But Robin knew this was not the end of it.

He knew the Bishop was a good friend of the Sheriff's. Sure enough, the Bishop told the Sheriff what Robin had done. The Sheriff vowed to make Robin Hood pay dearly.

Three

The Shooting Match

The Sheriff sent messengers across the land. They told of a great shooting match in Nottingham. The Sheriff invited the best archers. The grand prize? A golden arrow.

"I think I will go," said Robin to his men. "And win that arrow."

"But Robin," one of his men said. "People are saying the Sheriff has set a trap—just for you."

"That is all the more reason for me to go," said Robin. "I will not have the Sheriff saying that Robin Hood is a coward."

His men cheered.

How beautiful Nottingham looked on the day of the match! Brightly striped tents were pitched on the grass. Colorful flags and ribbons blew in the breeze. Peddlers sold fine

wares and delicious foods. Jugglers and minstrels strolled about.

Benches were set up near the shooting range. The Sheriff's seat was set higher than all the others. The poor people sat on the grass. But rich and poor, everyone wanted to watch the match.

The very best archers in the land had come. Giles Red Cap was there. The Sheriff's own archer, Clive of Leslie, was there. Then there was Adam of the Dell. And many others. Some were known. Others were not known.

The archers stood in their lanes. Some paced nervously. Others tested their bows.

The Sheriff arrived. Everyone bowed. His horse was saddled with the finest leather. Its bridle jingled with silver bells. The Sheriff himself wore purple velvet and many gold chains. He sat down.

The herald blew his horn. "Let the contest begin!"

The herald explained the rules:

"The target stands eighty yards away. Each man shoots one arrow.

The ten best archers shoot again. Each man shoots two arrows. The three best then shoot three arrows each. Of these archers, the best shall win the prize."

The archers stepped forward.

The Sheriff eyed them. Who was he looking for? Robin Hood, of course!

"Do you see him?" he asked his right-hand man.

The man studied the row of archers. No one there wore forest green. "Do not worry. We will find him among the ten best."

The archers shot. The ten best remained. The others left.

Of those ten archers, six were known. There was Giles Red Cap. Clive of Leslie. Adam of the Dell. And three more local men. Two

others from Yorkshire. Then there was a tall, fat fellow in blue. And a ragged one in purple who wore a patch over one eye.

The Sheriff was growing impatient. He said to his man, "Well! Where is Robin Hood?"

The man shrugged. He was most puzzled. "Six of these men we know. The two from Yorkshire are both too short. The stranger in blue is too fat. The ragged one in purple has a

brown beard. Robin's beard is golden."

"Then Robin Hood is a coward!" said the Sheriff. He was furious. Here he had gone to all this trouble to set a trap. And no Robin Hood!

By now the contest was down to the last three men. One was Giles Red Cap. Another was Adam of the Dell. The third was the ragged one in purple.

The crowd cheered as Giles and

Adam made their first shot. Then the stranger in purple shot. The crowd was silent. Then amazed when they saw his arrow strike. It was far closer to the bull's-eye than the other two!

The next round Giles and Adam shot better. Both came closer to the bull's-eye. Giles was the closest. The ragged one's shot was a bit off.

"Giles will win," the Sheriff said. "This one-eyed man has just been lucky."

The crowd watched. Giles came within a hair of the bull's-eye. Adam's shot was not quite so close. All eyes shifted to the stranger.

Boldly he stepped up. A hush fell. He mounted his arrow and pulled back the string.

With a hum, the arrow flew through the air. It hit the bull's-eye dead center! The crowd was too stunned to cheer.

"I have been an archer for twenty years," said Giles. He laid down his bow. "Never have I seen such perfect shooting."

"Nor I," said Adam. He shook his head.

The two men left the range.

The Sheriff came down from his high bench. He was beaming.

"Here is your prize," said the Sheriff. He handed the stranger the golden arrow.

"Tell me your name," he said.

"Jack of the Vale," said the stranger.

"Jack of the Vale, eh? You are the best archer I have ever seen," said the Sheriff. "Much better than that lily-livered coward Robin Hood."

The stranger stared at the ground. He gripped the golden arrow. His knuckles were white. But he held his tongue.

"Will you serve me?" the Sheriff asked.

"Never!" said the stranger. "No man in all of England will be my master."

The Sheriff sneered. "Then take your prize and be gone!"

Later that day the stranger in purple was seen in Sherwood Forest. He held the golden arrow high. The merry men clapped and cheered.

Then he tore off the eye patch. And he tore off the purple rags. Underneath was a suit of forest green.

"It will take me a bit longer to take off this walnut stain." Robin rubbed his beard.

The men laughed. Only they knew that it was Robin Hood who had won the golden arrow!

And what a jolly time they had that night! Robin told the story of the shooting match again and again. The men loved listening to a good story.

They shouted with laughter . . . until Robin got to the part where the Sheriff called him a lily-livered coward. The merry men were not so merry then. Nor was Robin Hood.

"The Sheriff has to know that Robin is no coward," said Friar Tuck.

"And that Robin carried off the golden arrow beneath his nose," added Marian.

"I think I have a good plan," said Little John.

Everyone listened. Robin smiled. He liked Little John's plan.

Later that same night in Nottingham, the Sheriff was having dinner with his men.

The Sheriff lifted his glass. "Let us drink to that coward Robin Hood! He did not dare show his face today."

Just then an arrow whizzed

through the window. It struck the table inches from the Sheriff's silver plate.

Everyone stared at the quivering arrow. No one said a word.

But what was wrapped around the arrow's shaft? A piece of paper.

The Sheriff's right-hand man unwrapped the paper. He read the message written on it. Frowning, he handed it to the Sheriff.

The Sheriff read it. And oh, how his blood boiled!

"Heaven bless the Sheriff today,
   say we in merry Sherwood.
For he did give the prize away
   to crafty Robin Hood."

The Sheriff pounded the table with his fist. Robin Hood had won again!

Four

The Rescue of Will Stutely

It was a beautiful day in May. In Sherwood Forest the birds sang. The bees buzzed. A band of the Sheriff's men rode along. They did not even notice the beauty of the day. They were busy searching for Robin Hood.

The Sheriff was tired of Robin Hood making a fool of him. He doubled the reward on Robin's head.

The Sheriff's men were eager for riches. They would search until they found Robin Hood. But so far all they had found were birds and deer and rabbits.

Why hadn't they seen anyone? After all, Sherwood Forest was the home of Robin Hood and his men. Where were they? Even now they were watching the Sheriff's men from their hiding places.

Robin knew about the Sheriff's reward. He was afraid it might lead to bloodshed. Robin liked adventure. He liked playing tricks. But he did not like bloodshed. He did his best to avoid it.

So he said to his men, "Hide. When they get tired of looking for us, they will give up and go home."

No one knew how to hide in Sherwood Forest better than Robin and his men. They blended into the leaves in their forest-green suits.

They sent messages to one another in bird calls. They moved with the silence of rabbits. Some said they had even dug tunnels beneath the earth, like moles!

This went on for some time. The Sheriff's men riding and searching. Robin and his men hiding and watching.

Then one day the Sheriff's men left the forest.

What was going on? Was it a trick to lure Robin and his men into the open? Robin sent out a spy.

"Will Stutely," he said. "Wear a disguise. Go to the inn and find out what our friend the Sheriff is up to."

Will Stutely was more than happy to go. Like the others, he hated hiding. He ached for an adventure. Little did he know what awaited him!

He put a hooded monk's robe over his suit of forest green and his sword.

He went to the inn called the Blue Boar. At the Blue Boar, Robin's men were welcome. So were the Sheriff's men. It was an ideal place to spy.

Sure enough, Will found a band of the Sheriff's men. They were drinking and talking loudly.

Will Stutely sat nearby. He kept his mouth shut and his ears open. Just a monk minding his own business.

But the innkeeper's cat knew he was no monk. He was her old pal who fed her table scraps.

She rubbed up against his leg. She mewed for scraps, pushing Will's robe up and up . . . until the forest-green suit showed beneath the robe.

One of the Sheriff's men saw it. His eyes narrowed. He came over.

"Hello, good father. Would you like a drink of ale?" he asked.

Will Stutely shook his head. He pulled down the hem of the robe. And shooed the cat away. He did not know it, but he was too late.

"Where are you going, good father?" the Sheriff's man asked.

"I am a pilgrim," said Will softly. "On my way to Canterbury."

The Sheriff's man said, "Oh? And since when do pilgrims wear green?"

With that, he yanked the robe right off poor Will Stutely!

Will reached for his sword. But the Sheriff's men had already surrounded him.

They were all smiles. Wait until the Sheriff heard! They might not have found Robin Hood. But now they had someone almost as good. One of

his not-so-merry men!

Marian was at home when she heard the news. A knight was visiting. He wanted to marry her. But Marian wanted to marry Robin Hood. Robin Hood did not think Marian should marry an outlaw. But Marian had ideas of her own!

The knight was shy. He did not know what to talk about. So he talked about the latest news.

"Have you heard? The Sheriff has

captured one of Robin Hood's men."

Marian choked on the apple she was eating. Her father pounded her back. "Are you all right?" he asked.

"No," Marian said. "I feel a little sick. May I be excused?"

Marian's father wanted her to stay and be nice to the knight. But Marian was already out the door.

A few minutes later she was saddling her horse. And on the way to Sherwood Forest.

"Faster! Faster!" she urged the horse. She had to tell Robin!

When Robin heard, he cried out, "Poor Will! If they hurt him, I will never forgive myself."

"Hurt him!" said Marian. "They are going to hang him tomorrow at sunset."

"Not if I can help it," said Robin.

He blew his silver horn. He told his men the bad news.

"Will risked his life for us," said Robin. "It's our turn to risk ours to rescue him. What do you say, men?"

"Let's do it!" the men shouted.

The sun was low in the sky. A big crowd had gathered in Nottingham to see the hanging.

Most people did not really want it to happen. Most people were poor and honest. The Sheriff was no friend of theirs. But Robin Hood and his men were.

The town gates swung open. The Sheriff's men rode out with the Sheriff leading them. They all wore heavy armor.

Will Stutely came next. He was riding in a wooden cart. His hands and feet were tied with ropes. How

pale he looked! And how very sad.

Will searched the crowd for a face he knew. Not one did he see. His heart sank. There were tears in his eyes. He hung his head so no one would see.

The last rays of the sun glinted on the armor. The men passed through the town gates. On the other side the gallows stood ready.

An even bigger crowd had gath-

ered out there. Will Stutely looked
up. In the distance he saw his be-
loved Sherwood Forest. And to think
he would never be seeing it again!

Once again his eyes scanned the
crowd. What was this? Little John!
And over there was Will Scarlet. And
who was standing not three feet away
from him? Robin Hood himself! Will
hung his head again. But this time
he hid a big smile.

The crowd pushed forward.

"Stand back!" the Sheriff shouted. "Give us a little room to hang this scoundrel."

"Stand back yourself!" Robin said. He thrust past two guards. Into the cart he leaped. He drew his sword and, in a flash, cut Will free of his ropes.

"Get him!" the Sheriff sputtered. He drew his sword. Little John lifted his staff and knocked the Sheriff right off his horse. The crowd cheered.

Then a battle broke out between the Sheriff's men and Robin's.

The crowd cheered and whooped as Robin's men beat back the Sheriff and his men. Back, back, back within the town gates. When the last man was in, Robin's men swung the gates closed. And pinned them shut from the outside with staffs.

The Sheriff and his men beat on the gates. They were locked inside. And it would be some time before they would be able to get out.

But neither the Sheriff nor his men really wanted to get out. They had had quite enough of Robin Hood and his merry men for now.

That night the merry men celebrated. Will Stutely was safe. Sherwood Forest was theirs to roam free in once again!

Five

The Sad Knight

It was a warm, sunny summer day in Sherwood Forest. There was plenty of food.

But the merry men needed gold. Gold paid for cloth of forest green. Gold paid for metal arrow tips.

This is how Robin Hood and his men got gold. They would hide in the forest and wait until a very rich-looking stranger passed. Then the men would leap out and stop him.

They were always very polite. They

would bid the stranger good day and ask his name. Then they would invite him to be their guest for supper.

The stranger would be fed and entertained in fine style. In fact, the stranger usually hated to say goodbye. Then the merry men would demand payment for the meal. Preferably in gold.

Did Robin Hood and the men keep all the gold for themselves? Never. They gave at least half to the poor. For this they were famous. Hated by the rich. But loved by the poor.

On this summer day Robin Hood and Little John went looking for guests. And gold. Robin went one way. Little John went another.

Soon Robin saw a stranger. A

knight! He was dressed well, but he wore no gold. And his head hung low as he rode.

"Stop, friend!" said Robin.

"Who are you?" the knight asked.

"What a good question!" Robin laughed. "Some call me kind. Others call me cruel. Some call me honest. Others call me thief. You may call me Robin Hood." He bowed low.

The knight smiled. "I hear good things about you," he said.

"Then come be my guest at supper tonight," Robin said cheerily.

"I would not hear of putting you out," said the knight.

"Not at all!" said Robin. "For you will pay your way. Believe me."

"Not this guest," said the knight. He held out an empty purse.

"Put your purse away," Robin said. "We will feed you anyway. For free. And try to cheer you up too."

Robin led the knight's horse toward the hideout. "What is your name?"

"Sir Richard of Lancaster," said the knight.

"And why are you so unhappy, Sir Richard of Lancaster?" Robin asked.

The knight told him.

Last spring the knight's son had been in his first joust. He had ridden against a great knight, Sir Walter of Fordham. By accident his son's lance slipped—and killed Sir Walter.

Sir Walter was a man with powerful friends. They demanded that Sir Richard's son go to prison. Sir Richard had to pay in gold to keep his son out of prison. He did not have enough gold. And so he had been forced to borrow. Now he could not pay it back.

"How much do you owe?" Robin asked.

"Four hundred pieces of gold," said Sir Richard. "If I do not pay it back by Monday, I will lose everything. My castle and all my lands."

By this time they had arrived at the hideout.

Little John had brought a guest too. And who do you think his guest was?

The Bishop! The very man who had given fair Ellen his golden chain on her wedding day. This time he had four horses loaded with bags. What was in those bags?

The Bishop stormed over to Robin.

"See here. How dare you let this man speak to me in such a way!" The Bishop pointed to Little John.

Robin Hood winked at Little John. "How was it he spoke to you?" he asked the Bishop.

"He called me a fat priest."

Robin Hood pretended to be shocked. "You don't say!"

"He called me a man-eating bishop."

"No!" Robin exclaimed.

"And he called me a grubby moneylender!"

Little John hung his head like a naughty boy. A very *big* naughty boy.

Robin turned to Little John and said sternly, "Is this true? Did you call His Lordship a fat priest?"

"I did," Little John answered.

"And a man-eating bishop?"

"Yes," said Little John.

"And a grubby moneylender?"

"I'm afraid so," said Little John.

Robin turned back to the Bishop. He shrugged. "Then I guess that is what you are. For I have never heard Little John tell a lie."

The merry men roared with laughter. The Bishop nearly choked with rage.

"Now, now, then," said Robin.

"Our guests must learn to take jokes. Come and meet your fellow guest, Sir Richard of Lancaster."

"If I did not know better," said the Bishop to Sir Richard, "I would swear you liked these thieves."

"I do like a good joke," said the knight. "No offense to Your Lordship."

The merry men laid skins upon the moss. They set up targets and had a bit of shooting practice.

Robin sat with his guests and watched. He was the perfect host. He made his guests laugh and feel at home. Even the Bishop felt quite comfortable.

Evening fell. Alan-a-Dale took out his harp and sang beautiful songs.

Then they lit torches. Food was

served. How delicious it was! And there was more than enough for everyone. Even the fat Bishop.

After dinner, Robin told the story of Sir Richard's son. How he had accidentally killed a knight. How Sir Richard might lose everything.

The men listened. Some were sad. Others were angry. All of them wanted to help Sir Richard.

"Maybe you could help him," Robin Hood said to the Bishop. "You are the richest holy man in England."

The Bishop stared at the ground in shame. He knew how he earned his gold. By cheating the poor. Still, he wanted to keep it for himself.

Robin asked Will Scarlet to unpack the Bishop's horses.

What riches! Bolts of velvet, silk, and golden cloth. Finally Will unpacked a very heavy metal box.

"Do you have the key, Bishop?" Robin asked.

The Bishop shook his head. He was feeling a little sick.

Robin nodded to Will Scarlet. Will drew his sword and bashed the box. It burst open. Out poured gold. Lots and lots of gold.

The merry men smiled and began to count the gold. More than fifteen hundred pieces!

"Relax," Robin told the Bishop. You may keep one third. I will take a third as payment for the meal. A third will go to the needy."

The Bishop didn't say anything. He knew he was lucky to be keeping a third.

Robin counted out five hundred pieces and gave them to Sir Richard.

"To pay off your debts. To save your castle and your lands."

There were tears in the knight's eyes.

"I swear I will repay you," he said. "And I will never forget your kindness."

It was a far happier knight who rode out of Sherwood the next morning. And a far lighter—and sadder—Bishop.

As for Robin Hood and his merry men? It had been just another summer eve in Sherwood Forest. And a merry one at that!

Six

Sir Guy of Gisborne

It was autumn in Sherwood. The air was crisp and fruity. The leaves had turned to fiery red and gold. Robin Hood and Little John went looking for a bit of adventure.

Robin went one way. Little John went another.

Robin Hood soon came upon a stranger. And what a funny-looking fellow he was!

He was dressed in horsehide from head to toe. Even his hood was made of horsehide. With the horse's ears still on it. He looked more beast than man.

But he was armed like a man. A deadly man. Heavy sword. Sharp dagger. A bow and arrows as well.

"Good morning," Robin said cheerfully.

The stranger was drinking at a stream. He pushed back his hood and wiped his mouth on his sleeve. Without a word he stared at Robin.

Robin shivered. He had never seen a crueler face!

"Good morning, I say," Robin repeated.

The man snarled.

"My, my!" Robin laughed. "Did you drink vinegar for breakfast?"

"Who wants to know?" the stranger growled.

"So you *can* talk! I was beginning to wonder. It is you who are the stranger in these parts. Tell me your name first. And why you wear that odd suit."

"Fool! I wear the suit to keep me warm and safe. For it is as hard as any armor. I am an outlaw. Sir Guy of Gisborne."

Guy of Gisborne! Robin knew the name well. He was the wickedest outlaw in all of England!

"Why have you come here?" Robin asked.

Sir Guy smiled. It was not a very nice smile.

"The Sheriff sent me to hunt down Robin Hood. You know what they say: Send a thief to catch a thief. I am to catch him. Or kill him. I prefer the second of the two."

Robin's head grew hot, but his voice stayed cool. "I happen to know this Robin Hood. And I don't think you have much of a chance."

Sir Guy shrugged. "I hear he is good with a bow. But I am better."

"I am not too bad myself," Robin said. "Show me how good you are."

Sir Guy started to set up a wreath of flowers for a target. But Robin stopped him.

"Allow me," he said.

Instead of flowers, Robin cut a single twig. He trimmed it and sharpened it and stuck it in the ground. One hundred yards away from where Sir Guy stood.

Sir Guy laughed. "The devil himself could not hit so small a target!"

But Robin was already stringing his bow. So Sir Guy did the same.

Three times Sir Guy aimed and shot. Three times he missed.

Now it was Robin's turn to laugh. "You are right! The devil himself missed the target! But now it's my turn."

Robin shot once. He missed.

Sir Guy snorted.

Robin shot again and clipped the twig. The third time he split the twig clean in half!

"There!" Robin flung down his bow. "That is how a real man shoots! And now get ready, Sir Guy. For I am Robin Hood. And you have finally met your match!"

Both men drew their swords. And how they fought! But in the end Sir Guy of Gisborne lay dead by the stream.

Robin Hood was angry. Sir Guy

was a bad man. But Robin Hood did not like to shed blood. Even the blood of a bad man. It was the Sheriff who had forced Robin to do it.

Robin took the horsehide suit off Sir Guy. He put it on himself and went looking for the Sheriff of Nottingham.

He did not have far to go. The Sheriff was waiting nearby.

Meanwhile, Little John had run into adventures of his own.

He had met a woman who was crying. The Sheriff's men had just taken her three sons. They were to be shot for killing a deer.

Little John knew that King Richard would not have minded. Not if the deer was killed for food.

"We are poor," said the woman. "And so very hungry. We had to eat."

"Where did they take your boys?" Little John asked.

"To the Blue Boar Inn," said the woman. "The Sheriff himself is there. He waits for Sir Guy of Gisborne to return from Sherwood Forest. With Robin Hood as his prisoner."

"That will be the day!" said Little John. Yet he was worried. Sir Guy was a bad man but a good fighter. Still, Little John had to help the woman before he helped Robin.

He dressed up like an old man and went to the Blue Boar.

Sure enough, the Sheriff was there. So were the three boys, tied together with thick rope. How frightened they looked! And how very young they were!

Little John burned with rage.

"Old man," said the Sheriff, "I will

give you a gold piece to shoot these three rascals for me. My own men cannot be bothered."

"I will do that," said Little John. Quickly he hatched a plan.

Little John walked the three boys to a big oak tree. He secretly cut their ropes.

"When I tell you, run into Sherwood Forest." He whispered to them, "Don't stop. Don't look back. No matter what."

The boys were terrified. But they knew they had a friend in this old man.

The Sheriff watched as the old man strung his bow. The old man took aim at the first of the three boys. Then he opened his mouth.

"Run!" he shouted. "Run, boys, run!"

And run the boys did! They ran
for their lives. Toward Sherwood
Forest and safety.

Little John turned. He aimed his
arrow directly at the Sheriff's heart.

"Don't move or I will shoot," said
Little John.

Inside the inn the Sheriff's men
had heard the commotion outside.

They sneaked up behind Little John and grabbed him. But it was not so easy. It took ten of the Sheriff's men to hold Little John down. Finally they tied his hands.

The Sheriff strolled over. He tore off Little John's disguise and smiled.

"What a great day for me!" he crowed. "Robin Hood will die. And so will his right-hand man—the big man himself, Little John!"

Little John just smiled. The three boys had gotten away safe and sound. His plan had succeeded. Almost.

"Robin Hood will not die," he said.

"Is that so?" said the Sheriff with an evil smile.

For just then Sir Guy of Gisborne walked out of the forest. The horsehide suit was red with blood. Whose blood?

Sir Guy held out a bow to the Sheriff.

Little John stared at it. He would have known Robin's bow anywhere.

"Robin Hood is dead," said Sir Guy.

Little John roared with rage—and sadness. What did it matter now if he died? Robin Hood was dead. What use was Little John's life without him?

The Sheriff was happy. "You can have whatever you want," he said to the man in the horsehide suit.

"I want to kill this big rascal with my own hands." The man pointed to Little John.

The Sheriff was surprised. Land, gold, a castle perhaps. But the life of Little John?

"Very well," he said. "He is all yours."

The man in the horsehide suit led Little John to that same big oak tree where the boys had stood not so long ago.

"You devil!" Little John snarled. "You killed my best friend."

"Easy, man," Robin Hood whispered. "I *am* your best friend."

Little John looked closely beneath the hood. His heart grew light as a feather. "Robin!"

"Shhhh!" Robin quickly untied

Little John's hands. "Your bow and sword are over there. Get ready. Get set. Grab them!"

Little John sprang for his weapons. Robin Hood threw off the horsehide hood. Both men faced the Sheriff and his men boldly, swords drawn.

The Sheriff cried out, "Robin Hood! You can't still be alive!"

"Oh, yes, I can!" said Robin. "And Sir Guy is dead. So will you be if you or anyone else tries to stop us."

The Sheriff and his men threw down their swords.

Robin and Little John backed up toward Sherwood Forest.

But the Sheriff made no move to stop them. He got on his horse and rode home. A broken man. For at last he knew what he should have known all along.

There was no man alive who could get the best of Robin Hood.

Seven

A Royal Visitor

There was great rejoicing! King Richard had returned from the Crusades. Rich and poor came to welcome him home.

Many people went to see the King at his castle. They wanted him to know what had happened while he was away.

The King listened. His face grew grimmer and grimmer. He heard the name of Robin Hood again and again.

Who was this Robin Hood? Was he a scoundrel? Or was he a saint?

The King knew one thing. He wanted to meet Robin Hood and judge for himself.

But how? He asked a friend.

"Take off your crown," said the friend. "And ride into Sherwood Forest. Sooner or later he will hold you up. And take at least half the gold in your purse."

"Thank you, Sir Richard," said the King. For the King's friend was Sir Richard of Lancaster.

Sir Richard said, "I hope you will be kind to Robin Hood. For he is a good man."

The King said nothing. But he did not look happy. Sir Richard of Lancaster feared for Robin Hood.

The Sheriff of Nottingham went to the King.

"I have heard that you plan to ride into Sherwood Forest. What a terrible idea! Robin Hood has no respect for law and order. For you or me. It's not safe."

"Not safe?" said the King. "I have heard he has shed no blood but that of Sir Guy of Gisborne. And we all know Sir Guy was a bad man."

The King looked at the Sheriff with sharp eyes. He had heard many bad things about the Sheriff.

"Perhaps you would like to ride with me to Sherwood?" asked the King.

The Sheriff grew pale. He backed away. "No, no, please!"

The King smiled to himself. He

would take care of the Sheriff later. But first things first!

The next day the King dressed up in the robe of a holy order. Six of his men dressed the same. Together they rode into Sherwood Forest.

"How foolish we are!" said the King when they had ridden well into the forest. "We did not bring anything to drink. I would give a hundred pieces of gold for one drop to drink."

Just then a man jumped out of a tree into the King's path.

He wore forest green. His beard was golden. His eyes were blue. And how merrily they twinkled!

"I heard what you said, Brother!" said the man in forest green. "And for a hundred pieces of gold you shall have all you want to drink."

"Who are you? And have you no respect for holy men?"

"Not a bit," said the man in green. "For while our good King is away, you holy men have grown as fat and rich as the Sheriff of Nottingham. My name is Robin Hood. You may have heard of me."

"I have heard you are a scoundrel," said the King. "Let us go in peace."

"I may be a scoundrel. But I am also a good host. And your host would not hear of you going thirsty."

"Then take my purse," said the King. "And give us a drink."

"Who do you think you are, the King of England?" asked Robin. But he took the purse. He counted out a hundred pieces of gold. And returned the rest to the friar. Then he blew into a silver horn.

Men in forest green came running.

The King looked around. How strong and healthy they looked!

"King Richard himself would be glad to have such bodyguards as these," he said. He was beginning to get an idea.

"Every one of us would give his life for King Richard," said Robin. "You holy men! You do not understand a man like Richard. He loves adventure. And so do we. We love our King!"

Robin and his men led the friars to the hideout. There they gave their guests something cool to drink. And set up wreaths for shooting practice.

The men took turns shooting. Robin went last. He decided to show off a bit for the guests.

"I will use only one arrow. And I will hit the bull's-eye. If I do not, Little John can strike me down."

Robin strung his bow. He pulled back the string. He let the arrow fly.

But what was this?

Something was wrong with the arrow. It landed in the bushes.

The men laughed themselves silly. But Robin Hood did not see the joke.

"You all saw that arrow!" he said. "It was bent. Let me try again with a straight one."

"Oh, no, you don't!" Little John wiped away tears of laughter.

"You are a bunch of cheaters!" Robin said. "But let my punishment come from the good friar here."

"Fair enough," said the King. "You owe me. For the money you took from my purse."

"Knock me down," said Robin. "And I will give it all back."

The friar rolled up his sleeve. What a stout arm he had for a friar! Still Robin Hood grinned and stood his ground.

The King threw his punch. Down went Robin like a sack of grain!

The merry men laughed and

laughed. They slapped their knees. They rolled on the moss.

Robin shook his head. He felt a little dizzy. He looked up at the friar. Then he joined the laughter.

"Little John!" Robin said. "Give this good man his hundred pieces of gold."

Robin got up. He dusted himself off. Then he heard someone call his name. Someone was running through the forest.

Sir Richard of Lancaster! What was he doing here?

"Robin!" Sir Richard stopped and caught his breath. "I said I would repay you someday. This may be the day. King Richard has returned from the Crusades. He himself is coming to find you. He means to bring you to justice. You must hide."

Suddenly Sir Richard stopped. He saw the friar. He knew that this was no friar. Down on his knee he went.

The friar threw off his robe. He wore a shirt with a red lion on it. Only one man in England wore such a shirt. And Robin Hood knew who that man was.

"Your Majesty!" Robin whispered. He too went down on one knee. "On your knees, men!" he ordered. "On your knees before good King Richard!"

The King said to Sir Richard, "Why have you come to warn Robin Hood?"

"You are my King," said Sir Richard softly. "I owe you my loyalty. But Robin Hood is my friend. And I owe him everything."

Then Sir Richard told the King

what Robin Hood had done. How he had taken gold from the Bishop. And given it to Sir Richard to pay his debts.

The King listened in silence, nodding. Then he said, "I have heard many stories about Robin Hood. Even in the Holy Land, men spoke of your good deeds. I didn't believe them then. But now I think I am beginning to."

Robin Hood did not say anything.

"Robin Hood," the King went on. "Don't you think it is time you came out of Sherwood Forest?"

"I will do as you wish, Your Majesty."

"I wish you and your men would stop being outlaws."

"Yes, Your Majesty."

"I will pardon you and your men, but only . . ." King Richard stopped.

Robin waited.

"Only if you will come and serve me. Help me rid the land of these bad men. Help me rule England justly and fairly."

"I would be honored, Your Majesty," said Robin. "And so would we all."

The King drew his sword. He touched Robin on each shoulder.

"Arise . . . Sir Robin, earl of Locksley."

The merry men stood up and cheered!

Robin Hood had gone down on his knee an outlaw. And risen a free man—and a nobleman at that!

Never was there such a feast as the

one they had that night in Sherwood Forest—with the King himself as their guest of honor.

It came to pass from that night on, Robin served his King as an honest citizen. But even as a nobleman,

Robin never forgot the poor and honest folk. He continued to fight for their rights. And they in turn told wonderful stories. Stories of the bold and daring deeds of the man known as Robin Hood.

Annie Ingle and her five brothers discovered Robin Hood as children. They pretended that the woods near their Maine home was Sherwood Forest. Just like the wandering minstrels and storytellers of long ago, they retold, invented, and acted out tales about Robin Hood and his merry band. In this adaptation, Ms. Ingle gives Marian the same spirit as the Marian she played at being so many years ago.

Domenick D'Andrea illustrated *Black Beauty* in the Step-Up Classics series. He has created covers for many history and adventure books, especially stories about the American West. He lives in Stratford, Connecticut.